The Tiny King

Taro Miura

Lancas
Bowra
Pres

Once upon a time, in a land far, far away,
there was a Tiny King.

The Tiny King lived all alone in a big, big castle.

He had an army of big soldiers with long spears and stern faces. Wherever the Tiny King went, the soldiers marched behind.
Left, right, left, right, left, right.

He could never finish so much food all by himself.

The Tiny King had a big white horse.

But he was so tiny and the horse was so big
that he fell off every time he tried to ride.

The Tiny King had a big, big bathtub.
It even had a water fountain.

But splishing and splashing all by himself
was never much fun.

The Tiny King's bed was a big, big bed.
But he slept in it all alone every night.

The Tiny King was so sad and so lonely
that he never slept very well.

Then one day,
the Tiny King fell in love with
a Big Princess and asked her
if she would be his Queen.

She said yes!

And soon they were
happily married.

Not long after, the Tiny King and the Big Queen were blessed with children—lots of children.

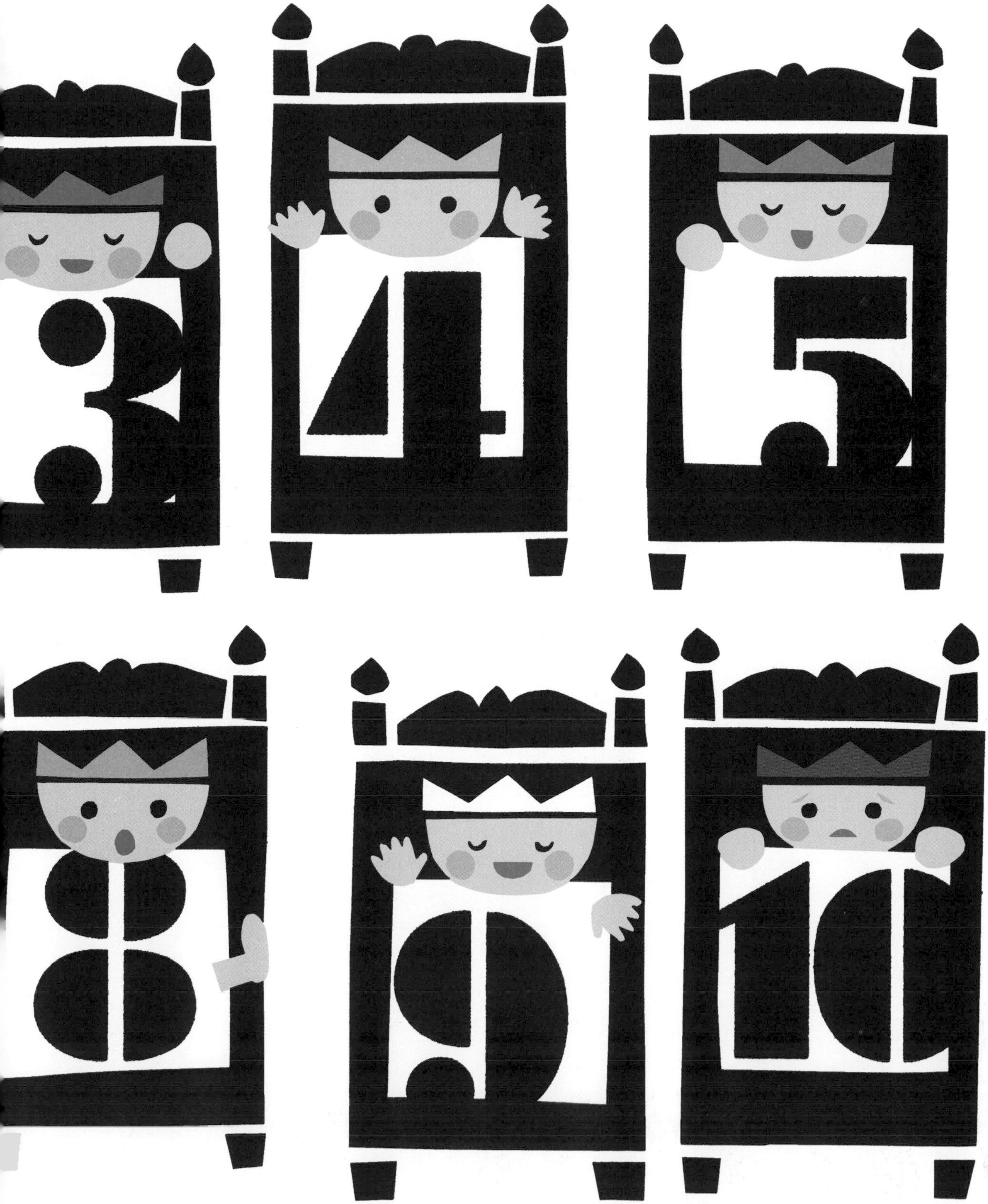

The Tiny King was so happy that he sent
his army of soldiers home on holiday.
They all marched off – left, right, left, right –
back to their families.

Now the Tiny King's castle no longer felt so big.
The children ran around, laughing and playing
all day long.

The Tiny King and his
family gathered round
the big table every day.

Together, they had no trouble finishing the enormous feast of delicious food.

And look! The big white horse pulled the Tiny King and the Big Queen in a carriage while the children rode on his back.

Here they are, on their way to a picnic.

Now bath time was a real riot!
The Tiny King and his family splished
and splashed together every day.

And what about the Tiny King's big, big bed,
where he had been so sad and so lonely?

Well, when everyone snuggled up side by side,
it was just the right size.

And the Tiny King slept soundly at last.

Look, here he is, fast asleep.

Good night, Tiny King.